FLOATI[NG]
ELEPHAN[T]

Jay Sonty

For my friends and family, who have supported and encouraged me.

Sometimes when I'm by myself
and I'm looking in the sky,
it seems the most unusual clouds
are the ones that catch my eye.

I see caterpillars and dragons,
fishes, cars and giraffes,
but clouds that look like floating
elephants make me smile and laugh.

I see them riding bicycles and
lying on their backs,
I see them doing somersaults
and jumping over cracks.

Sometimes they're playing hide and seek or peeping out of other clouds, sometimes they pull each other's tails and are trumpeting out loud.

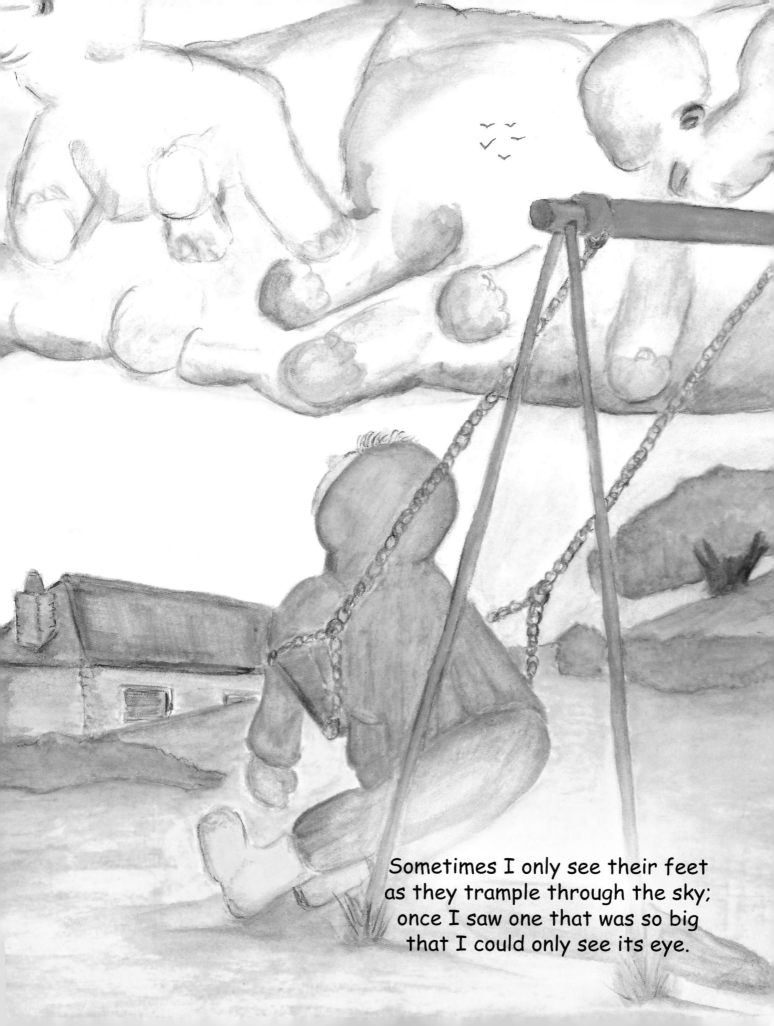

Sometimes I only see their feet
as they trample through the sky;
once I saw one that was so big
that I could only see its eye.

I saw one that had a long, long trunk and one that had five legs,
I've even seen a floating elephant that was eating scrambled eggs.

I've seen them jumping helicopters that
are zooming through the air,
I've seen one that had giant ears and one
with flowing, curly hair.

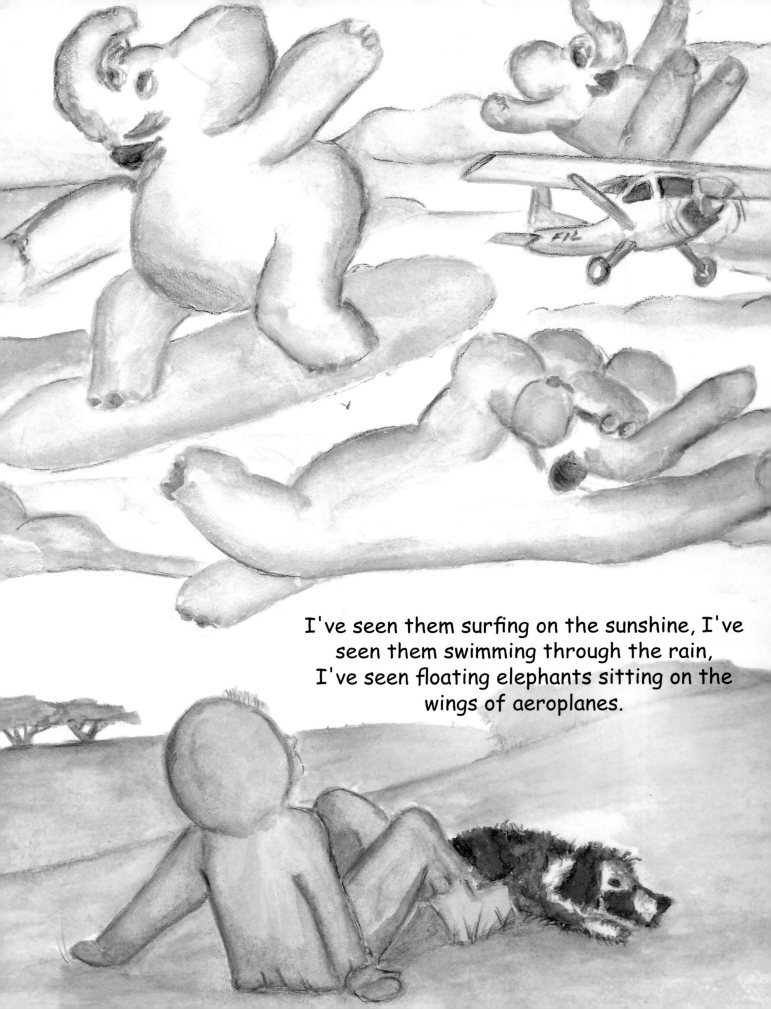

I've seen them surfing on the sunshine, I've seen them swimming through the rain,
I've seen floating elephants sitting on the wings of aeroplanes.

It often makes me wonder
how they get up so high;
are they made of clouds or dreams or
fluff or are they just made out of sky?

And every day when I go outside, I know that they'll be there, those funny floating elephants are always floating round somewhere.

When it's sunny and I'm outside,
I know I'll never be alone
because up in the sky above me
there are elephants that roam.

And I still see caterpillars, dragons, fishes and giraffes but my favourites are floating elephants... they will always make me laugh.

You can draw the cloud animals you've seen in the sky
on these empty pages

You can draw the cloud animals you've seen in the sky
on these empty pages

You can draw the cloud animals you've seen in the sky
on these empty pages

You can draw the cloud animals you've seen in the sky
on these empty pages

You can draw the cloud animals you've seen in the sky
on these empty pages

You can draw the cloud animals you've seen in the sky
on these empty pages

You can draw the cloud animals you've seen in the sky
on these empty pages

You can draw the cloud animals you've seen in the sky
on these empty pages

Printed in Great Britain
by Amazon